Each Puffin Easy-to-Read book has a color-coded reading level to make book selection easy for parents and children. Because all children are unique in their reading development, Puffin's three levels make it easy for teachers and parents to find the right book to suit each individual child's reading readiness.

Level 1: Short, simple sentences full of word repetition—plus clear visual clues to help children take the first important steps toward reading.

Level 2: More words and longer sentences for children just beginning to read on their own.

Level 3: Lively, fast-paced text—perfect for children who are reading on their own.

"Readers aren't born, they're made.
Desire is planted—planted by
parents who work at it."

—**Jim Trelease**, author of
The Read-Aloud Handbook

For Jon and Jamie

PUFFIN BOOKS
Published by the Penguin Group
Penguin Books USA Inc., 375 Hudson Street, New York, New York 10014, U.S.A.
Penguin Books Ltd, 27 Wrights Lane, London W8 5TZ, England
Penguin Books Australia Ltd, Ringwood, Victoria, Australia
Penguin Books Canada Ltd, 10 Alcorn Avenue, Toronto, Ontario, Canada M4V 3B2
Penguin Books (N.Z.) Ltd, 182–190 Wairau Road, Auckland 10, New Zealand

Penguin Books Ltd, Registered Offices: Harmondsworth, Middlesex, England

First published in the United States of America by Viking Penguin, Inc., 1988
Simultaneously published in Puffin Books
Published in a Puffin Easy-to-Read edition, 1993

3 5 7 9 10 8 6 4

LIBRARY OF CONGRESS CATALOGING-IN-PUBLICATION DATA
Ziefert, Harriet.
Dark night, sleepy night / Harriet Ziefert;
pictures by Andrea Baruffi.   p.   cm.—(Puffin easy-to-read)
ISBN 0-14-036538-9
1. Animals—Juvenile literature. 2. Sleep—Juvenile literature.
I. Baruffi, Andrea. II. Title. III. Series.
[QL49.Z48 1993]
591.1'88—dc20   92-47290   CIP

Puffin® and Easy-to-Read® are registered trademarks of Penguin Books USA Inc.
Printed in the United States of America

Reading Level 1.5

DARK NIGHT, SLEEPY NIGHT

Harriet Ziefert
Pictures by Andrea Baruffi

PUFFIN BOOKS

Dark night
Quiet night

Starry night
Sleepy night

Everybody sleeps.

Snakes sleep in walls.

Bears sleep in dens.

Woodchucks and skunks
sleep under the ground.

These rabbits sleep
above the ground.

Look at a tree!

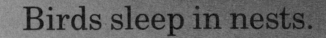

Birds sleep in nests.

Squirrels
sleep
in holes.

Look again!

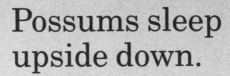

Possums sleep
upside down.

Ladybugs sleep
in tiny cracks.

Horses sleep standing up.

Dogs sleep lying down.

Bats sleep
with their eyes open.

Cats sleep
with their eyes closed.

Turtles and frogs
sleep deep in the mud.

Fish sleep at the bottom
of the lake.

Chickens sleep.
Pigs sleep.
Cows sleep.
Goats sleep.
Everybody sleeps.

People sleep
in all kinds of beds.

High beds...

Low Beds...

Little beds....

Soft beds...

Hard beds...

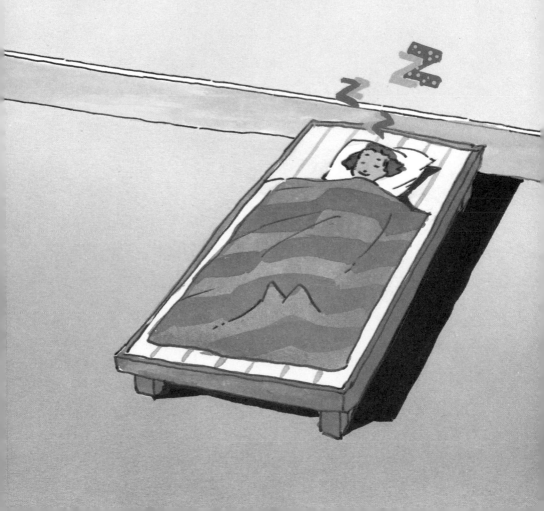

Where do you sleep?